My Pussy

tells her story

by

Julie Topper

Pink Panties Press

Other titles by Julie on Amazon

The spider stockings
Art School goth
Parlour games
The chavs are coming
Nights out with the girls
Cheating on my boyfriend
Don't treat it like a banana
A Week in the life of an escort
Boyfriends have their uses
A change of style
The Masquerade club
Mousing around
Hermaphrodite
Gym slips
Night Rider
Dogging it
Double Vision
Barmaid in blue jeans
The Boys in the Band
Art School goth gets casting
The Job in Hand
Blondie and the Four Fannies
A wild week in Benidorm
The School of Venus
Sex wi' a Glasgow accent
My new boyfriend
Linda Lovesit erotic writer

Contents

Chapter 1

First encounters

Julie and I have been together her whole life, but she only really got to know me a few years ago. She became aware of me when she was twelve or so, but we only became truly acquainted when she was seventeen. Before that, she was all over my neighbour Miss Clitty, who got all her attention.

Every night she was out there, playing with Miss Clitty and me not getting a look in. I know those two get on well, but I'm the girl she really loves. To prove it, I decided to write this little book.

Julie can be a bit wayward, changes her mind all the time. One minute she's after some guy, and the next she's totally finished with him. She changes men almost as often as she changes her panties, and I'm glad she does that every day!

I go with her everywhere, but often she forgets all about me. I have to lie down there pretending to be asleep, waiting till she deigns to think about me. I do have my moments, however, when she is all over me, and I get lots of attention. At times like that, I come into my own.

We first became seriously acquainted when she was on holiday with her Mum and Dad. She had brought along one of her human friends, Pam. Mum and Dad thought she was a good influence, a nice sensible girl. How wrong they were! Pam was well acquainted with her special friend, who had tasted the delights quite a few times.

They took us to a place called Torremolinos. 'Lots of beach', it should be called. Mum and Dad were quite protective, not allowing us to go out at night to the town. Quite right too, from their perspective, but not from mine. I was feeling like I was going to miss out. Instead, Pam and Julie were allowed to walk along the beach in the afternoons, without Mum and Dad looking over their shoulders every moment.

So that fateful afternoon, Pam and Julie were sitting on the beach, putting on lots of sunscreen, and watching the other people pass by. Two Spanish boys saw them and came over to talk. They spoke English rather badly, which amused Julie. After a while standing awkwardly, they sat down and began trying to impress the girls. Julie and Pam were really entertained and loved getting the attention from the boys.

They sat around for an hour or more when one of them said, in rather fractured English, "Why don't we go up to the shops and I'll buy you two an ice cream."

So they went. The boys led them up some small lanes and passageways, till the girls had no idea where they were. Apparently, no ice cream was coming soon.

The boys took them down this dark lane, and they stopped half-way, where it turned a sharp corner. One of the boys pinned Pam against the wall and began kissing her. She eagerly pressed herself against him. Julie didn't know what to do. The other boy was not so pushy, but eventually, he put his arm around her and pulled her to him. His mouth was on hers, and she had the lovely sensation of tongue kissing. That totally woke me up. A bit of that definitely gets me excited. Sure enough, his hands were soon on her hips stroking the outside of her thighs, only a few inches away from me. I began to swell up, and a torrent of my sticky juice poured into me. I was hoping that Julie would let him at least touch me. His hand moved down the front of her bikini bottom and patted me. What a lovely feeling. Julie's heart was pounding, and her breaths were getting faster.

Pam being a much naughtier and more experienced girl, had let her boy pull her bikini down to her ankles and gave him full access to her cunt. I was so jealous of that cunt, brazenly opening her lips to his fingers. Julie and I could hear Pam and her cunt having fun.

Julie's guy was determined to get a bit of what his mate was getting. He tried to pull down on the sides of her bikini, but Julie resisted. God, I'm going to miss out, and here's me all excited and ready for it. He finds another route, pulling the material of her bikini to the side so that my lips were out into the fresh air. I was so slippery. Thank God she was going to let him finger me. One of his fingers found my labia and opened me up. Another finger followed, and he began stroking up and down my slit. I was in heaven. Poor Julie was conflicted. This was so nice, but she didn't want to lose control. She was, at that time, the opposite of me. I wanted her to lose control and let it all happen. I had lived long enough now without tasting the pleasure I was clearly made for. 'Bring it on,' I thought.

A few feet away, Pam was getting fucked. He was inside her, standing up, and thrusting away, her cunt taking his full length. It really excited me being so close to getting the same, but I knew Julie wasn't going to give in. I could tell by the way her body was tensing that she wasn't going to relax and give her boy what he wanted. I resigned myself to enjoying the fingers which were now rather ineptly searching for the entrance. I would have loved to have opened wide and showed him exactly the way in, but Julie was keeping her legs tight together. Still, I was getting fingered in my slit, which was so nice.

Things were getting serious with Pam. Her boy was now slamming her hard against the wall with every stroke. He gave out a little cry, and it was all too quickly over. I would have given anything to change places with her cunt and taken the lovely cream we cunts so desire. It's our reason for being, after all, our purpose in life. 'One day I'll get lots of that," I thought, 'But, sadly, not today.'

As soon as he finished, he wanted to go. He talked to Julie's guy in Spanish, pulled his fingers out of me, and they ran off up the alley, laughing and shouting something in Spanish. It sounded a bit like "Puta, perra, marrana." We had no idea what they meant, but it was probably not very complimentary.

So Julie and Pam had an adventure, and so did I. I wasn't exactly a virgin any more. That night in bed, Julie lay back and opened her legs to expose me naked. Her fingers explored my lips, and I began to moisten again. She pushed her fingertip into my opening a few inches. She was remembering what the Spanish boy had done that afternoon, and so was I.

I was expecting her to do it the full way, when suddenly she abandoned me and moved a few inches North to her then best friend. I had to lie still while Clitty took her pleasure. To make things even worse Julie was at her again only ten minutes after they had cum, for a second go.

'One day my time will come.' I comforted myself. I will be all grown up like Pam's cunt.

Chapter 2

The name's the game

You know people call me lots of names. I'm used to it now. I have some polite names and others that are only said in wild moments of passion.

Julie prefers to call me 'Fanny', a nice soft and gentle name. I think it really suits me. It suggests a nice open-hearted girl, always with a smile on her face. Someone friendly and happy to meet others. Not too deep or serious. One who is the life and soul of a party. I do like parties, you know! I'm at my best then, showing myself off to the guys.

Now 'Cunt' is gutteral and not so sweet and sticky as fanny. When I am a cunt, I am in bad girl mode. Cunt is more abstract. It's more a general term. Guys use it when they are not really thinking about Julie but only about me. We become somehow detached from each other in the man's mind. There are lots of cunts in the world, and men think of us as being much the same. It's our form they are thinking about and not all the rest of Julie, her rather delicious thighs, her smooth rounded breasts, or her delightful little face with its engaging and captivating smile. All those they dismiss from their mind when they think only of me as a cunt. Cunt is something they get inside and have fun in, to hell with bothering about what fun Julie is getting. Quite often she likes these moments, perhaps when she's drunk, and she just becomes a cunt. Guys realise she's in that sort of mood and are quick to take advantage. It's great for me, cos I get the fun without Julie getting in the way. When I am a cunt, I absorb men, I take them into my slippery embrace and make them groan and gasp. They have to work hard to make me happy. I can be a hard taskmaster. When they are a bit frightened of my power, they diminish me in their minds by calling me 'cunny'.

'Vagina' is my proper name. Miss Vagina - used in formal occasions when I meet doctors. Their interest in me is a bit remote, and perhaps a little too clinical. Usually, they won't even touch me without putting on gloves, and they prod about inside or push some things up to take their samples. I have gotten ill a few times. Nothing serious, but on occasions, I have been decidedly itchy and uncomfortable, especially when Julie was sitting down. When this happens, Julie goes to the chemist's and buys some useless sticky, smelly cream, and I have to put up with that for a few days till she decides to go the doctor and get some real medicine. So it isn't always easy being a vagina. We have our difficulties. I will gloss over the monthly madness that Julie's ovaries imposes on me. I mean, why do those two ovaries have to have a cleanout once a month. Have they not heard of spring cleaning? Humans do that once a year, why can't those devils, the ovaries, take their lead from humankind. They lurk up there, deep inside Julie, and make my life a misery for a few days. Don't they realise Julie is on the pill? It's not just me that suffers, Julie has a bad time too, often having to turn down offers for a night out, and instead it's a night in with ibuprofen and nursing a hot water bottle. Not much fun for her! They should be more considerate.

'Pussy' is a silly name. It makes me laugh when they

call me that. That's why it's in the title of this book. When you call me 'pussy' you avoid my reality, my primal nature. Instead, the picture of a warm, snuggly cat, with soft fur, comes into your mind. Though I am not a cat, I do like being stroked and often purr with delight, but I can assure you, cats would not put up with what I sometimes get done to me. It's not a name that Julie uses for me. She doesn't use it often in her books. I, myself, find it a bit childish and diminutive. It makes me seem bland and inoffensive when I can assure you I can really upset guys big time. I'm no soft pussycat, but someone to be reckoned with.

I even have a classical side, hardly used nowadays. No man has ever called me that when Julie was about. I am the amazing 'Mound of Venus', the little hill where the Goddess of Love sits. I can imagine those naughty Roman centurians conquering Europe and making much use of the Mound of Venus, perhaps even without asking the Goddess' permission to enter her sacred temple. The less poetic Romans would just call us 'Vulva' and knew how to open our lips and take their pleasure - it's still a Latin word but much less elevated than Venus's hill.

I am not exactly a simple girl, I have many different aspects, and those provide me with even more names. My most obvious aspect and the most visible, is my lovely tight and curly hair. Thus I am the 'Minge', the 'Muff' and the 'Beaver'. Not long after Julie first discovered me she became a bit too adept with the razor, so I lost my lovely locks, all because it was the fashion, and you have to go along with what men wanted. Men want me to be all smooth and what they think is feminine, but they miss out. Happily, as she has got a bit older Julie has put away foolish things, and discarded the razor, and I am back to my natural form.

Another obvious part of me is the lips that enclose me and keep me safe and warm when I'm sleeping but open up when Julie gets excited. That's my Roman Vulva, but in these pagan less classical times, I am called 'Slit', 'Crack' or 'Gash', evocative perhaps but not exactly poetic or polite. Julie often calls me her slit, so I take that as her pet name for me. I must say I love it when they slide their fingers up and down between my lips. Julie does that when she is frustrated or has missed out on some midnight fun with a guy. 'Gash' and 'crack' are a bit too common for Julie to use, but I've been called that a few times by uncool men with a restricted vocabulary. We fannies do get called crude names quite often in the heat of the moment.

Moving on from my outer lips to my true centre, the bit all men desperately want to visit, because of their intense excitement I get called the 'Hole', the 'Fuck-hole' or 'Shag-hole'. The number of times I've heard that in my grown-up life, well I could write a book about it. When I hear that, I know that Julie is long gone from the front of their mind, and only my lovely warm wet interior fills their thoughts, though they're probably not thinking much at the time. At those moments, I like being called the 'hole'. It exactly describes me, does it not? They plough, fuck, ride or shag me, and for a few seconds, I am their's, their own lovely hole. They worship me for a minute or so before I drain them of their energy. I am like a big black hole among the stars eating them up one after the other.

So that's some of my names. I've heard others, but these will do for now. I'm Julie's favourite fanny, I know she has had her fingers in a few others, but she always returns to me, especially when she feels excited.

We cunts are not simple, are we? We have lots of different sides to us, and so we get called different names.

Without us, the world would collapse, as men went mad, and poor woman would have no fun at all.

9

Chapter 3

The hairbrush

A month or so after the Spanish incident, Julie was still puzzling over the experience. It had been a bit disturbing, but at the same time, she couldn't forget the feeling of those fingers playing with her.

I could only wait my time. I knew she would have to come to terms with me eventually. I expect that happens with all women.

So it was late one night, when, having given Miss Clitty a few minutes stimulation, Julie decided to see what delights I could offer. I felt her fingertips in my slit. They slid up and down, up and down, slowly, even a bit tentatively. I gave her a little burst of pleasure to keep her at it. I began to fill with my stickiness. Julie shifted her position in the bed to get a better angle. I heard her breath deepen, and blow air out of her mouth in quick gasps. I had her trapped now. She circled my entrance with her fingertip. I pressed out some more of my lubey juice, and she started playing with it. I was so keen to feel her finger inside that I made her hips thrust out, and then it was done.

She was a bit surprised, I think, but wanted to find out more. I relaxed and felt at least an inch of her finger slip inside me. I won't be alone any more after this night! I didn't need to thrust her hips anymore, she would do this herself.

She spread her legs, so I was wide open and explored as far in as she dared. Then the little darling slid in another finger beside the first. She began pulling forward quite roughly. My first real fun. 'This is my life now, getting this every night,' I thought, 'I will be so grown up soon.' She was now pulling forward very rhythmically, taking deep gulps of breath. I felt her other hand move to Miss Clitty. A big wave of pleasure poured through me. I tightened my opening in time with her pulls. Delicious it was. Clitty kept Julie working away, and it was only a few minutes before I felt a delightful spasm of pleasure as she squeezed her legs tight together and thrust her hips up and down about ten times.

I think she was a bit shocked by the intensity. I certainly was. I knew it would be good, but not as good as that, and this was only two fingertips. What delights must await me when she lets a man slide into me.

I was hoping this would be a nightly occurrence, but Julie seems to have held back and stubbornly continued with her clitty obsession. Maybe once a week she would explore me in the same way. This wasn't really enough for me.

This all changed one night. She had Pam round in her room one evening, and they were having woman talk. Pam was telling her all the details about what men were like. I listened attentively, trying to commit it all to memory. The rather precocious Pam even confided that she often used an artificial dildo. What an idea! I had never thought of that, and I don't think Julie had either.

After the all-knowing sex expert, Pam, had left, Julie went a bit quiet. I could tell she was looking amongst her things for something, maybe she needed it for work tomorrow.

We got into bed, and she assumed the legs wide

position. Lovely, I thought, tonight another fun night for me getting fingered. It started that way and, without her bothering with Miss Clitty, she was straight down to fingering around inside me. I got nicely wet and was settling down for a good night, when she withdraws her fingers. I am deflated, she will go back to Clitty I expect. Julie is so fickle with her affections.

She is reaching out to the bedside table. I feel something a little bit cold pushing into my slit. It is hard but smooth. It spends a few seconds circling against my opening, then with a sudden movement, it pushes deep into me. I am so shocked that I can't quite take in the experience. Julie gives out a rather loud groan and begins moving the wooden handle of her hairbrush in and out of me. Julie and I are having actual sex, the way it should be, for the first time. She drives the hairbush handle faster and faster. This is how it will be from now on. She won't give up this feeling any time soon. I excel myself with lubrication. The dirty bitch has it the full length in. About four inches, I estimate. There are more depths of me to explore, but that will be for another day. I am now just a sex machine as the handle goes rapidly in and out. Julie is now so excited, her breathing fast and deep. She is totally in another world, a couple of dozen faster strokes then one big hard thrust and I pulse and throb as a big wave passes through her body, this time including me. Oh, delight of delights. How wonderful it is to be alive. This is what Miss Clitty must have been getting for all those years, the lucky bitch.

Julie is a bit disoriented. She has been totally surprised at the intensity. She checks me to see if she might have done me some damage. Damage! We cunts are tough. One day I'll be taking hour-long poundings from her randy boyfriends. What's a few minutes with a hairbrush beside that.

That was a good few months ago. She graduated from the hairbrush handle to a soft pink latex dildo that Pam leant to her, no doubt already well broken in by Pam.

One night Julie got adventurous. Instead of lying on her back, she turned on her front, and when the dildo was inside me, she held the end in her fist, so it was rigid against the bed and began to move herself and me up and down on it. It seemed much more physical for her. I was just enjoying the sensations of it moving inside me, and the bumping against her fist as she pushed right down. Miss Clitty was getting involved, whether she liked it or not. The bed creaked as she rode herself off, and with all her excited groans, no doubt, Mum and Dad would have heard. They never said anything of course.

This was the way things went for the next few months. Life was good. Julie was having lots of orgasms and was developing a new confidence in herself.

And I was now wide awake and looking for more experiences.

Chapter 4

A drunken quickie

My first big break came at Angie's party. Pam and all the crew were there. The party was quite crowded, with young men as well as the girls. I could almost taste the testosterone. People have to drink at parties, otherwise, they stay all quiet and miss out on the chat. Julie, not at all used to alcohol, had rather underestimated the power of raw vodka. After a few too many of those, she was getting a bit unsteady when she stood up, so some nice guy invited her to sit next to him on the sofa. She graciously accepted.

He turned out to be a bit of a charmer. I could tell he was totally interested in Julie. He poured out his banter of jokes and silly stories on her, while gradually slipping his arm around her and pulling her close to him. She was flattered, of course. She was still drinking more vodka, so was almost unable to think straight at all. When he started kissing her, she just lay back and enjoyed the feeling, little suspecting it was merely the prelude to some more intense pleasures. One of his hands was on her knee. Well, it started there, but quite quickly moved up her legs under her skirt. I sensed it coming closer. Julie could not resist the wish to open her legs a little. His hand moved on till it found her panties. She reckoned this was going to be a repeat of the Spanish incident, and she was not wrong. Except in this case, the man was very much more experienced than those Spanish boys.

Pushing aside her panties, he quickly found my entrance. I was only just beginning to get slippery, but he pressed his way in. Julie, still getting kissed, opened her legs even more, and I felt his two fingers slide into me. This was like the dildo but even more exciting. The dildo was rigid and immoveable, but his fingers moved about within me, testing, probing, pressing on me, pulling forward, a whole new repertoire of experiences for me and Julie.

After ten minutes or so of this, he starts trying to get Julie to her feet.

"Let's go through the back," he says, "It's quieter there."

Julie is not so sure. She liked being on the sofa, but she didn't want to disappoint the man, so she lets him lead her, a bit unsteadily, through to the back bedroom.

He sets her down on the side of the bed, and she flops back. Everything is spinning around a bit. She wants it to stay still. His hands are up inside her skirt, and her panties are then on the floor.

She knows she can have full sex there and then. She is undecided. I give her my vote for a 'yes'. He leans over her.

My God, his prick is out. I sense it close to me. I am so ready now. Julie is still in two minds. I am not.

I feel prick for the first time sliding in my slit, picking up my juices and testing Julie. I give her a big surge of pleasure. He presents his cockhead just at my opening, teasing me without entering. In that instant, Julie decides. She lifts her legs and opens them wide. He knows the sign and instantly thrusts forwards into me. I can't help tensing and grabbing at it with my muscles, but he pushes against me, slides right up inside me and holds there for a few seconds.

He begins moving slowly inside me, kissing Julie all the time to keep her sweet. I hear him whispering something to her. This is the first time I ever hear the 'Cunt' word. I am no longer a virgin as he starts more serious thrusts all the way up inside me then pulls down to my opening, almost, but not quite, coming out. He is definitely well skilled at that, he knows his way around a cunt, exactly how far to go.

I am making acquaintance with his cock whose head likes to seek out my deep soft bits. If it had its way, it would just stay there, but the cock's shaft wants to keep moving. This is what life is about, this lovely rhythmic, slippery, slidy movement.

Suddenly things get very serious as the man starts going very fast. I hear him say the word 'cunt' over and over. Julie is totally excited, and lifts her legs even higher up. To her, it's a shag, but for me, it's a terribly intimate kissing embrace of a lovely cock that is exactly made to fit inside me. I grip and squeeze it as it moves, so we sort of sing a sex song to each other. It tells me it's going to have me soon. I feel the friction of its final fast strokes as the man grunts and pushes his cockhead far up inside me. It pulses inside me, and suddenly there is the first warm spurt of his cream. It floods my upper cavity, but more and more spurts come as he thrusts away to his finish.

Julie wasn't expecting that. She lies still, in a bit of a daze, her head full of the experience of sex. I, on the other hand, am full of man juice. It tastes quite sweet. I will have to get used to this. No doubt it will happen again and again now Julie and I have been initiated.

The guy goes off satisfied, leaving Julie, legs open, on the bed. She sits up and searches for her panties. She looks down at me and sees I am leaking out his spunk.

"Shit!" she says. Then internally to herself, 'No condom. What an idiot. I might get pregnant.'

The door opens, and Pam looks round. "He gone?"

She comes in and sits beside Julie. "You lucky bitch," she giggles, "I fancied him."

Chapter 5

Double date

Next morning Julie was at the chemist's getting a pill to make sure she wouldn't become another unmarried mother. She also, rather embarrassedly, bought a packet of condoms.

So I'm hoping she is ready for anything.

After a few weeks, I realise she is a bit conflicted by what had happened. I was expecting this would mean more action for me, but quite the opposite. In her bed at night, she preferred the comfort of Miss Clitty. I realised she was blaming me for what had happened at that party. Maybe I should have put up more resistance when the cockhead first pressed into me, I could have grabbed it tight and not let it go any further, but I didn't want to resist. I let myself go slack and welcomed him in. I was just being myself. Doing what I'm good at. That's what I'm made for, after all. It was really Julie that made the decision by lifting her legs and giving the come-on.

Over the weeks she relented, forgiving me, and the lovely, almost nightly, visits from Mr Pink Dildo resumed. He's not the same as pulsing hot flesh, but I was getting more experience, so when she got back to men again, I would be well ready for them.

* * * * * *

Pam is being a bad influence. Well, bad as far as Mum and Dad would think, but good from my perspective. She comes round and sits on Julie's bed and tells her things that excite and amaze her. I lap all the details up. There is so much to this sex thing isn't there.

She has some pictures on her phone which she shows to Julie, mostly of guys or of Pam's nights out in clubs with her friends.

"You should come out with us sometime," Pam says. "We have great fun."

She gives Julie a totally naughty look. "Plenty of guys. Plenty of cock."

Usually, after one of Pams visits, Mr Dildo was out, and sometimes I would have him two or even three times in a row. Great times for me but I sensed that Julie was getting too frustrated.

It wasn't Pam, however, that got me my next encounter with lovely fleshy cock. It was a girl in the shop Julie worked in. I heard her asking if Julie would like to go on a double date with her. She fancied this guy, and he had a reasonably nice mate, so they could all go out together. Strangely, Julie didn't hesitate, and it was set up for the weekend.

It needs alcohol, doesn't it. Well, the guys they were with definitely believed that and came prepared with plenty of drinks money. They took the girls to a noisy bar with rock music playing and tried to chat them up with shouted conversation. Julie's downfall, clearly, is vodka. She fails to appreciate its power.

The guys took them off in a taxi. Julie was all giggly by now and had no idea where they were going. It turned out to be the flat of one of the guys.

As soon as they got in, the girl from the shop and her man went off to his bedroom, leaving Julie on the settee with his mate. He wasn't exactly a ten out of ten, but I could tell Julie wasn't really bothered. Within a few minutes, they are kissing and not long after he gets them both lying side-by-side along the settee. His hands are all over her. Julie keeps her legs closed. I sense the hormones rising. And not just the hormones! Julie feels his hard cock inside his jeans, pressing against her legs. She is so curious that she reaches down and feels it through the cloth.

Bed creaks and unmistakable sex sounds come from the bedroom. That girl's fanny is certainly having fun. She's definitely more experienced than me. Listening to this has quite an effect on Julie. She twists round on the settee till she is lying on her back. Her guy undoes his trousers, and the wonderful sex machine comes out, with all its big veins pulsing. There is no way Julie is not having that.

She opens her legs, and he begins rubbing the delicious hard thing against her panties. I feel its shaft pressing the material into my slit. This stimulating friction goes on for a few minutes, then Julie reaches down and tries to pull her panties off. As the man is lying between her legs, he has to help. Well, it's now an offer he can't refuse. No man would, I expect. There I am, opened up and totally ready for it. I am saying, even shouting, 'Yes, yes, yes' and so is Julie.

The lovely pulsing shiny head is sliding in my slit, pushing my lips apart. It finds my hole, and I know its dying to get in, when Julie says very forceably "Condom."

"Oooh. You have to?"

"Yes."

"It's much nicer without," he pleads.

She pulls her legs together to make the point.

He isn't going to argue. I hear the snap as a wrapper is opened, and there is a bit of fumbling as he puts it on. He laughs nervously, trying not to spoil the mood. Condoms make cocks feel much smoother. I like the sensation of smoothness. They also seem, from my experience, to delay for at least a few minutes, the guy from spurting. At first, I loved the sensation of the spunk being pumped, but I also have come to appreciate the cock lasting a bit longer, especially when its going at full speed.

He needn't have worried. Julie and I are both desperate. There will be no turning back. Her legs are wide open again.

It's in, and it's lovely. The shaft pistons in and out of me. It is so smooth. Julie's legs are all over the place as she enjoys the feeling, The guy has problems staying in me as she is moving about so much.

"Babe, lie still and take it. Leave the moving to me."

He is back in the saddle that is her open legs. I'm the centre of that saddle, and he takes me rather fast and furious. Julie is a good girl now and lets him have his ride. His shaft works up and down me so fast, always moving, never staying still. I hardly have time to feel its shape. It's a total blur. I am so excited that I let so much juice flow that Julie and I both hear the so explicit sloppy sex sound. I am now definitely a sloshy cunt. It's obvious, that just as with her first guy, this one is not in any way interested in Julie. All he wants is cunt, and that is me. At that moment, I'm the one he loves, not her. He would stay inside me for the rest of his life if he could.

But sex is not like that. The spunk relentlessly rises in his shaft. I now know a little bit about men, or rather their cocks. I can sense something change in its rhythm. A sort of pulsing low down the shaft, then the big thrust in and the pumping. I feel a blob of it gather in the condom.

The guy cries out "Fucking hell." And it's over.

He slides himself out very carefully. His cock lost its

stiffness right after the pumping. He makes sure the condom comes away safely. He's definitely used sheaths before.

The two of them lie on the settee. Now he begins relating to her. He wants to know if she came. She tells him 'No'. He looks a bit disappointed.

She says, "It's not important. I loved it anyway."

"You wait a bit girl, and I'll give you one, definite."

Why do guys always say that? It's their ego that's hurt, I think. Their prick is totally happy with the outcome.

Naughty noises from the bedroom again. Julie and her man smile.

"She's in for it tonight," he says. "And so are you."

As they listen to the pounding next door, his fingers go down between her legs. He finds my lips and locates my hole. I am so well lubricated now that the fingers slip in without any pressure in his part. He twiddles them about for a few minutes. It's nice but not exactly exciting after the fast fucking I have just had.

Something is changing. He's moving about on the settee. Then he twists Julie round, so she is sitting upright. He's good at this and manages to keep his fingers twiddling inside me as he repositions her. He now is kneeling in front of her.

"Legs wider," he orders, as his face comes down to meet me with a sloppy kiss. His tongue licks up and down my slit, and he nibbles at my lips.

'This is different,' I think. 'Where's it going?'

He only spends a minute or two lapping up my juices, before moving a few inches North. I might have thought so. It's Miss Clitty's turn. I giggle to myself. 'I wonder what she will make of this, she's not had the tongue before.'

He's good! He keeps his fingers inside me, marking

time like a soldier. I purr with a quiet delight. Miss Clitty is telling Julie that this is so good, that his lips and tongue are almost as good as her fingertips. Not totally true, of course, he's not exactly ace at getting the rhythm and speed right as far as she is concerned. But I don't think she is actually complaining.

This goes on for a few minutes until Julie starts making seriously sexual groans. The man knows he is on a winning streak and gives up the slow stirring inside me, replacing it with intense rapid thrusts of the two fingers inside me. 'This is more like it. Real sensations.'

Miss Clitty is beside herself, sharing her waves of delight with me. I am ashamed at all the bad things I have said about her over the last months. She is my colleague now in this sex business. We will work together from now on. Julie's pleasure is what comes first.

She tries to lie still, but it's getting a bit overwhelming for her.

"Don't stop, please, please don't stop," she calls out.

"I'm with you babe, don't worry," he says and speeds up the fingering.

Well, that did the trick for me, and Miss Clitty concurred. It only needed twenty seconds or so of the fast fingering, when Julie let's out a long scream and cannot control her legs which thrash about in the air.

"You bitches love that, don't you." He is right pleased with himself.

Julie is all hot, intensely red in the face and sweaty. Her man now moves her onto her back again. He is totally roaring hard again. He puts on a condom and thrusts deep into me.

"Shagging after a cum is so good. You're so easy and loose," he says and selfishly takes his sexual fun in her.

She just gives in, not really feeling much, well not in a

intense way. Miss Clitty is quite out of the game. It's left to me to finish him off. I am definitely 'cunt' now and more likely just a 'bit of hole'. For him, he's finished with Julie, and only thinking of how much fun he can get in my slippery tube. He intones 'Cunt, cunt,' as he comes to his climax.

Chapter 6

The bells toll

I won't describe all the times I had in the following few years. Those two times established her libido. She went on the pill, and I became a regular feature in her life. After a while, she didn't even need the vodka, but could have it totally sober, even in the afternoon. I became a total expert in cock. She was such a naughty girl in her late teens and early twenties that I tasted hundreds of them. She came to have such a reputation among her circle of friends as a bit of a wild girl, that guys who had been with her would talk about how easy I was to enter.

She had some boyfriends, but they usually lasted only a few weeks or months. I liked the boyfriends, especially getting used to the same cock. Once I get to really know a cock I can find neat ways to please him. I can tense my muscles and give him a squeeze if he likes that, or just go totally slack if that's their thing. When we get really well acquainted and so comfortable with one another, I can open up my deeper passages to him that others haven't ever tasted.

Just as I would be getting used to one boyfriend, Julie would be off spreading her legs for some really inappropriate man, and the boyfriend was dumped.

*　*　*　*　*　*

There was one night, however, I need to talk about. It was what humans call New Year. That didn't mean much to me, one day is just like another, but somehow it's special to them. They need lots of drink to celebrate this New Year business.

My mistress was out drinking with her friends going from one bar to another. Eventually one of them suggests they go on to a party she's invited to. I am so sure I will get some use tonight that I lick my lips at the thought and moisten them just a little.

They troop off to the address and find a rather small flat crammed tight with people. Bodies rub against bodies it is so cramped. Julie gets a bit fed up with the crush and is about to leave, when a rather neat younger guy comes up to her and starts the chat-up. She flirts outrageously and, as they stand in the crush, he begins gently stroking her bottom. Now I'm certain that I'll be having some fun later.

The chat-up progresses well, and Julie's face is all flushed, with drink as well as growing libido.

"Heh, it's too crowded in here," he says. "Fancy having a party at my place? It's just around the corner."

"Sure."

"Meet you in the hall here in five, I'll go and make some phone calls to my mates. I'll get the party going, so we can watch the bells on the telly at 12.00."

'So. A party just for me. How sweet,' Julie thought.

It was a bit more than five minutes, but he was there eventually. He took her arm, and they went out into the street and began walking to his place. They passed by a row of shops. He pulled her into one of the doorways and began kissing her.

'Wow, he's eager,' she thought. 'Even if there's no actual party I will have a good time with him.'

While he kissed her, his hands took hold of her hips,

and he pressed her against him.

'Yeah, definitely eager.'

She reached a hand down, seeking the front of his trousers.

"Roll on the New Year," he laughed.

They went on to his place. A run-down student-type flat. He put the gas fire on, and pulled the settee and seats back to clear a space. In this, he piled up some cushions.

He switched the telly on, and it was only fifteen minutes to midnight. He motioned for Julie to lie on the cushions and then joined her. I began to lubricate in anticipation.

His hand was up the skirt, and Julie relaxed as his fingers found me.

"Are you the sort of girl who likes a real party?" he said.

Julie giggled non-committally, thinking he meant that he wanted to have sex with her.

"You've got that look about you, you know. Bit of a banger."

He had his fingers inside me now, softening her up.

"I've got four of my mates coming over," he said."I don't have to let them in, but if I do, then it's a real party. You know what I mean."

Julie thought for a moment.

Did she want this? All four of them? I sure did.

I tried to influence her. I managed to give a little twitch, hoping she might respond.

The bells were striking on the telly.

"God, Julie, let me slip in, just as it goes midnight."

She laughed and as a reply slipped off her panties and lay back.

'What a wonderful ritual,' I thought. 'Seeing in the New Year this way.' I wondered how many other cunts were about to get it as well. If I could smile, I would.

With the first strike of Big Ben I felt his stiffy slide into me. Julie giggled. He gave just a few strokes then pulled out.

"Fancy me and my four mates," he asked.

"Why not," Julie replied.

If I could cheer, I would.

He went and got some drinks. He got out a skimpy bathrobe, and Julie undressed and put it on.

"Just lie there all provocative like," the guy says. "My mates will love that."

About ten minutes go past when there is a knock at the door, and four young men come in, probably all only about eighteen or nineteen.

They stand around a bit embarrassed.

Eventually, one of them asks, "Where you find this one?"

One of them whispers quietly to another, "Hope she is well drunk." The two of them giggle with each other.

Another one asks their host, "You had a go yet?"

"Well, I've warmed her up," he makes a dirty gesture. "Come on, Julie, let them see what you have."

She opens the bathrobe.

There are gasps all round.

"Heh, she's a great find," one of the boys says. "Nice tits. Brilliant thighs."

"Right, you know the score, anyone who wants a go has to strip off. Those who just want to watch can sit at the back on the settee."

They all remove their clothes, down to their T-shirts.

"I found the bit of bird, so I get first go," our host says.

He climbs on top of Julie and whispers in her ear, "Don't worry, we've done this before a few times with an old bitch that lives upstairs. We're experts. You won't get hurt."

I feel him entering. He doesn't bother with foreplay. He takes his fun in me with short stabbing sort of strokes. Julie is unmoved, but I'm not. His thrusting pulls more juice out from inside me and makes my slit all sloppy wet. I'm definitely going to need that tonight.

It's all over in just a few minutes. He pulls out, and another guy takes his place. This cock likes to go a bit deeper in. Julie is quite impassive, just lying there taking it. I sense she has not quite got into the sex yet. I will make sure she does. This second guy likes working it right deep into me. He is not very long, so his body rams against Julie's crotch with each stroke. That wakes her up sexually, and she gives a few groans.

"The bitch loves it," one of the guys says.

"Ram her hard, man, give her it hard. They love it that way," another suggests.

The second guy doesn't last long either before I feel his spunk filling me. Two loads. It will come gushing out soon.

They don't wait around, as the third of them gets on top right away. It's one cock after another, with no breaks for me.

"God, you're fucking wet, bitch. Total legspreader." He rides away at full speed, as the others did.

I'm becoming aware that I am getting puddled.

"Look at her fanny, she's creaming up," I hear one of the guys say.

'Well no surprise there, mate, after two loads and all this stirring,' I think. If I were Julie, I would be such a bad mouth, but she retains a silence, with just an occasional gasp as the guy on the job seems to do something special with his cock.

"Heh, I want to ride the slut now, she's a fucking

creampie," one of those left out so far says. "She's so much better that the fat old ride from upstairs."

"Two of you hold her legs up so we can see her cunt taking the prick," someone else shouts.

Julie is definitely beginning to feel the sex. She was cool to start with, but after three cocks worth, it is getting to her.

Now they've held her legs up the fourth guy can get really deep into me. His cockhead finds the nice really soft bit around my cervix, and only a few thrusts later he cums to his climax.

There's only one guy left now, the youngest and the most inexperienced. He takes me very tentatively, slowly exploring my interior space.

"Come on, ride her, give her a good one, she's gagging for it. Girls need it fast, man."

They all start chanting "Shag her! Shag her! Shag her!"

He obliges, giving me his piston with full throttle up. I can't help making that rather disgusting, sloppy sound that guys love to hear as he works himself up to his cum. I'm totally creamed, and it's got all churned up and leaked out.

Having finished, he pulls out. They let Julie's legs fall back down, and she re-positions herself so that her legs are open with her knees bent.

"Is that all you've got, guys?" she teases them.

"Look at her, she's covered in spunk."

Two of the guys make their apologies and leave. So it's only three left. They get down to second helpings. Without the crowd noises and having lost the raw edge of their sex drive, they each do it very seriously and deliberately. I give Julie two massive orgasms.

*   *   *   *   *   *

So that was that New Year party. Only six months later she got banged again, this time at a rock concert. A guy gave her some 'e', and she danced around in front of the stage totally blissed out. Julie can be a bit over-impressed by guys in black leather jackets, and when it started to rain, without thinking, she went back with him to his marquee tent. There she met some of his fellow motor-bikers, and they all had a good night. I am insatiable, you know.

Chapter 7

The husband

Things went well for me for the next few years. I got to taste a number of cocks and experience the different ways they liked to use me. Julie was definitely popular with a number of guys, and I benefitted from that.

Then I gradually came to realise that one guy was getting to know Julie rather well. There followed a year of me being the favourite of a particular cock, who came to monopolise me. I didn't mind, as it was really nice not to have to go for weeks without being shagged. I was getting it regularly, about three or four times a week.

There were, of course, a couple of returns to previous cocks, usually when Julie was a bit drunk. I must say it was nice to have a bit of a change.

Eventually, things settled down, and Julie was married. We moved into her husband's house, and for nearly five years, everything stabilised. A routine developed. Most nights, his cock would slide into me and would vigorously take its pleasure. I did enjoy knowing that, when night came, it was more than likely that I would be put to use. I became so important in the relationship between the husband and Julie. His cock was especially active on Sunday mornings, sometimes surprising itself and me by having three goes. Lovely that was.

Some time in the sixth year of this marital bliss, Julie

took me to a party. I sensed her rather over-indulging in the free vodka. She stayed on till all the other guests had left. I must say I was expecting something to happen but was totally surprised at being taken to the back bedroom to be used, rather roughly by three of the cocks at the party. I had cock moving in me continuously one after another for over half an hour. Both Julie and I were ecstatic. I was totally creampied, used over and over, two or three times, by each of the guys' cocks. Julie was outrageous, telling the guys that she had really missed getting it like this for years.

One of them said, 'Well just phone us up whenever you fancy another go'.

And she did.

It was probably my fault. I was getting a little bit bored with the husband's routine. Not that it wasn't nice, but it lacked a sort of edge to the excitement. His cock took me for granted and had become quite selfish, hardly ever bothering to check if I was getting the full fun. That night at the party, I had passed on to Julie lots of waves of pleasure. Instead of keeping them to myself, I let her have the full blast of sexual energy that was being given to me by the cocks. I did this to make her aware that I wasn't entirely satisfied with the status quo.

So there followed a number of months when Julie took me back to that flat, usually on a Saturday afternoon, and we enjoyed the three young men almost as much as they enjoyed me.

After five or so of these visits, other things began to happen. Julie would arrange to meet the guys individually, often after work, and they also introduced her to other friends of theirs. I was becoming a bit of a slut. Not that that particularly bothered me, I don't share the same morality as men and women do. A cunt fears not being used, being neglected, side-stepped and ignored. I suppose I felt I should assert myself to Julie, make her aware of my needs, the tedium of her husband's cock gushing itself into me without giving me much pleasure.

This exciting period lasted a bit less than a year, before everything crashed down and things changed. It seems that the hubby found out about the younger men and got totally furious. Julie and I were grounded. We were not to go out at night, and had to get back home as soon as work finished. Sexual privileges were withdrawn for some weeks. Julie returned to Miss Clitty. Those two would have long bath's during which they would please each other. I was neglected, blamed somewhat unfairly, I thought, for creating the situation.

Hubby restrained himself for a few weeks, but one night his cock could hold things in no longer, and I felt Julie's legs being opened and, without any warning, I was getting rammed rather forcefully. It took me a few seconds to lube myself, but I welcomed the intensity of the ride. I'm not sure Julie felt the same, but she accepted it. I agreed, it was a bit selfish and one-sided.

After that, hubby would just expect the panties off whenever he felt like it. Julie complied dutifully. I suspected she was trying to save the marriage and that she was expecting these selfish demands would eventually diminish, and we would all return to the cosy normality and stability we enjoyed before. I'm not saying I didn't have some great moments. Hubby's cock was often so intense that I got totally into the sex. Julie however, had erected a kind of barrier and would not let me pass on my enjoyment to her. So it was great fun for me, but I knew this situation could not continue and there was a crash awaiting us all.

The end came when hubby announced he had taken a

new job in a city some 300 miles away. He was renting a flat down there and was vague about whether he would visit very often.

Weeks, months went by with no visit from him. Julie had a few phone calls, but mostly they were about domestic and financial matters.

I began to sense Julie getting restless. Her nightly encounters with Miss Clitty were not entirely resolving her sexual energies. One night I caught her toying with her phone, thinking to call one of the young men who had unwittingly led to the break up. She stopped herself from pushing the last digit of the phone number.

I was getting seriously worried about her.

Chapter 8

I enter a parallel universe

After the breakup with her husband, I might have expected Julie to have been seeing the young men more often, or looking for other male partners, but she withdrew into herself. I sensed her depression. She seemed to have lost her libido, and what were once almost nightly stimulations for me, got rarer and rarer, so much so that I and Miss Clitty also fell into a kind of depression, and hardly ever troubled Julie with our desires.

Julie needed to talk and share her pain and hurt with someone else, so one day, she got up the courage to phone one of her woman friends.

*　*　*　*　*　*

The next evening she went round to see her friend Carol. They sat on Carol's settee, sipping large brandies while Julie gradually unburdened herself. Carol was definitely a sympathetic listener. She nodded as Julie described each detail of the breakdown. It became obvious that Carol was not very tolerant of men. She found them overbearing, selfish and always holding women back from doing what they wanted. She herself had never married and seemed rather anti-men.

After much soul-baring and perhaps a little too much

brandy, Julie broke down and started crying in long slow sobs. Carol put a comforting arm around her and pulled her close for a warm cuddle.

"Thanks, that makes me feel a bit better. A bit more human." Julie tried to fight back the tears. "I'm so wound up right now, Carol. My life is all messed up because of this."

Carol squeezed her tighter. "It will be okay. You will heal, it takes time, that's all."

Julie responded to the warmth of her friend, cuddling up close to her, till her face was up close to Carol's. Julie's cheeks were wet with tears.

Carol wiped them away with her hand. "You look so vulnerable, but also so attractive. You are so beautiful that I can't understand why that stupid boor of a husband of yours would leave you."

She kissed Julie's cheeks and licked around her eyes. The two gazed deeply into each other's eyes for a minute or so, and I felt the familiar surge of hormones.

Julie and Carol were now kissing rather fiercely. I began lubricating disgracefully, being programmed to get ready to accept cock in this sort of situation. Suddenly, clothes were coming off, and the two of them went off into Carol's bedroom and lay naked side by side on the bed.

Carol's right thigh pushed its way between Julie's legs opening them. Carol pressed her thigh higher up till I felt it rubbing against my lips.

Julie groaned. "I miss it so much. You have no idea."

"I'm here now, Julie. Just leave things to me."

Her knee moved back, and I felt Carol's fingers gently working up and down my slit. They felt each lip in turn and pressed on them sensitively. I got even more slippery wet.

At this point, I would have been expecting a prick to

slide in, but instead, Carol's fingers began exploring inside me. Julie spread her legs wide to make it easy for Carol.

Then followed an amazing five or even ten minutes of total excitement for both Julie and myself. I had never been fingered like this. Carol was so much better at this than men. I've had lots of fingering, but this was totally exciting. Her fingers were so sensitive and knew exactly how to please me. Julie lay back and just gasped, taking her fun. After a few minutes, I realised I would give Julie a massive cum if Carol kept doing this.

She did, sensing Julie's heightening tension by working faster. I was soaking wet and making sex noises as her two fingers played with me. Suddenly two turned to three, forming a tight bundle which pushed in and out of me like a fat cock.

Julie groaned and groaned. Her legs went right up into the air. Now Carol was using all four fingers, forcing them right up inside me.

Less than a minute of that and Julie and I came to a massive orgasm. As I climaxed my muscles tightened and clamped round Carol's magic fingers, pulsing a few times as I passed these spasms on to Julie's body.

Julie lay back with her legs wide and pulled Carol on top of her. They lay in a tight embrace.

Carol's cunt was so close up against me that it began kissing me as Carol gently moved her hips. Her cunt was smooth and hairless. It pressed into my wetness. Her clitty, now quite swollen, tasted my juices and explored up and down my inner lips.

"It's my turn now," Carol whispered and began moving her hips so that her cunt could rub and ride itself against me. Her pace gradually increased, and I began to sense what this strange way of having sex was about. I was a quick learner, and also very frustrated after a few lonely months that I just gave in to what was happening and tried my best to please Carol.

"Wider open, darling," she said, "Just for me, please."

Julie obeyed, and Carol's cunt rubbed against me even faster. Later, I found out this is called tribbing. At the time I didn't care what it was called, it was so nice. As seems to apply to all kinds of sex, it gradually got faster and more insistant. Carol was away in her own sexual space. I was just providing her with a warm wet trench to work out her orgasm. She came rather gently, taking much, much longer than a man would. Her cum seemed to go on and on for nearly a full minute. She groaned loudly as she ploughed each stroke of her orgasm into me.

The two of them lay back, seemingly exhausted. Carol even appeared to fall asleep for a few minutes. Julie lay there considering what had just happened. Her hand came down to feel me and realised how wet I was. I had been having so much fun that I had totally forgotten about Miss Clitty. Julie hadn't. She began giving her what she needed.

Carol woke up from her micro-sleep. "Heh, you still not satisfied!"

She moved down in the bed till her mouth was close up against me. Her tongue tip found Miss Clitty's sensitive head, and the sex thing started again.

*　*　*　*　*　*

The two of them stayed awake till about two in the morning having sex in different ways, with so many orgasms I lost count.

39

Chapter 9

The ride

Julie 'saw' Carol a few times over the next weeks. Carol was primarily the active partner which suited Julie well. She needed to get used to this new sexual awakening.

She became worried about becoming a little bit too attached to Carol, who she knew was 'seeing' other women.

When Carol went off on holiday for three weeks, Julie decided to try and find other female partners. She knew there would be bars and night clubs for lesbians where she could meet other women. She expected it would be a bit intimidating walking alone into such a bar for the first time, but she resolved to try it at least once.

So the first Friday night when Carol was away, Julie chose a pub whose clientele, she had heard, were primarily lesbian. Julie didn't feel the term 'lesbian' applied to her. She felt herself to be more of an explorer in a sexual world previously unknown to her.

I was pleased with this development. I really needed much more stimulation and new partners. I wanted to know all that a cunt like myself could experience. I sensed there was a whole ocean of sexuality to be explored. If Julie had decided to abandon men, then together, we had to find all that women could offer. I was ready for the challenge.

'What on earth to wear?' That was Julie's main problem that Friday evening. Laid back, or in your face? It was easy with men. You went out totally obvious, even tarty, and that would get their attention. Was it the same with women on women encounters? 'What signal should I be sending?' she puzzled.

After much turmoil and trying on various outfits she opted for a just above the knee, loose dress in soft pink, with sheer flesh-coloured hold-ups. On top a rather feminine light jacket.

She looked at herself in the mirror a few times. Eventually, she felt it would work and called a taxi at about 8.30.

She wanted to get their early before the pub would get too crowded, in the hope that she might be able to chat to a few people.

As she thought, the venue wasn't too busy. She found a seat at the bar and ordered a double vodka. She might need a few of these to get through the night. After only a few minutes, a rather thin young woman came up to her.

"Haven't seen you here before. You from out of town and just passing through?"

Julie was unspecific saying she just fancied making some new friends.

"Come, let's go and sit at my table and chat," the young woman said.

She was called Suzie and worked in a wholefood shop. Julie had made up the story that her relationship had broken down, and she was looking to broaden her horizons. She didn't say that her relationship was with her husband.

Some of Suzie's friends came over and introduced themselves. They were all in their early to mid-twenties.

Julie began to feel a bit out of things as they talked about music, fashion and stuff she had little knowledge of. She wondered if this had been a bit of a big mistake. She was ten years older than these young women and felt part of a different generation.

Suzie must have sensed this as she said, "Let's go and have a private chat, say outside. It's not too cold."

Taking their drinks, Julie was on her third vodka, they went and stood in the street just outside the bar.

"I really like you, you know." She smiled, "You have lovely eyes."

Her hand reached down, found Julie's free hand and held it, her fingers stroking the back of Julie's hand.

She brushed her fingers down the side of Julie's hip. "Come on, let's go somewhere. I really fancy you."

The pulse of hormones began to flow towards me. 'I'm going to get some fun tonight,' I thought to myself.

"My place then," Julie said. "I'll get a taxi."

"If it's not far we can walk," Suzie suggested.

On the way to the flat, she told Julie her life story, or as much as she felt able to reveal.

When they got in, Julie realised she had not even thought that she would be bringing a woman back tonight. There was a pile of the clothes she had earlier tried on, heaped up on the back of a chair.

Suzie reached out and picked up a tan leather mini skirt. She giggled "If you had worn that, half the bar would have been after you. It so makes a statement."

Julie was unsure exactly what sort of statement it would have made. There was much to understand about this lesbian stuff.

Within a few minutes, they were on the sofa, kissing rather intensely. Suzie was an extremely good kisser. Julie put her arms around Suzie and pulled her down, lying back so that Susie was on top of her. Julie's dress became all pulled up to her waist, so that Suzie was lying between her legs.

"Mmmmm, warm thighs."

Suzie pulled away from her intense kissing and looked Julie straight in the face. "Let's go to bed, get naked and have a lovely long cuddle."

In the half-minute it took to get there, my lips were totally moist.

"I smell your sex," Suzie whispered. "Makes me want to taste it."

With that, her head was down close to me. Her tongue began licking the outside of my lips. Julie was so excited that she spread her legs wide and I opened up like the petals of a flower.

"So shiny wet," Suzie said.

Suzie's tongue lapped in my slit, tasting my juice. She stayed there for some minutes, before moving up again to kiss Julie on her lips.

"You taste divine, don't you."

Julie tasted me and decided she would have to agree.

Suzie rolled onto her back and assumed the same position, exposing her fanny for Julie to worship.

Julie wasn't very sure about this. She knew it would happen eventually. It goes with the lesbian lifestyle.

She tentatively explored Suzie's outer lips, before taking the plunge and slipping her tongue between them. It tasted a bit more bitter and acidic then she was expecting, but like a good lover, she did not show this.

Suzie wanted her to turn round. Being not quite sure what was wanted, she let her lead, eventually realising it was to be a sixty-nine. Suzie was below, with Julie's head between her legs while Julie was on top straddling Suzie's head. I was wide open and in a way kissing Susie on her mouth. I flooded with more juice as the tip of Suzie's tongue penetrated into me. This was good fun. Miss Clitty was also being pressed against Suzie's chin. We both gave Julie a surge of pleasure, and a truly marvellous thing began. Julie started to thrust me up and down against Suzie's face. It began gently, but as I got more excited by these movements, each thrust of which, sent a twinge of pleasure through me, Julie began to ride faster. Soon I was being ground vigorously against Suzie's face. Suzie, lying underneath me, began to shake her head from side to side, which made the movements even more delicious.

I began to become aware that Julie had now lifted her head from between Suzie's legs allowing Suzie's hand some space to work on her clitty. Julie was relentless now, selfishly determined that I should have as much fun as I could take. This was as close to me getting a good shagging, as was possible without a man. Julie was now riding Suzie's face as fast as a man rides a juicy cunt, or a jockey approaching the final furlong. Suddenly I felt the cum rise in me. This was set off by Miss Clitty, who obviously was very close to her big moment. She sent out pulses of total pleasure to me and to Julie's body, and as Julie let out a loud groan, we all came.

Julie pulled herself off of Suzie, moved head-to-head and began kissing her so strongly. Then the poor dear began crying, her tears wetting Suzie's face.

"It's too much," Julie sobbed.

"Wow! you're so intense. Are you always like this?" Suzie wondered.

They lay together for ages gently stroking each other and every now and then getting into a little kissing session.

"When I first saw you in that soft pink dress, I thought you were totallyfemme," Suzie said, "But you sure know how to dish it out. You must meet some of my friends. I'll get you invited to some parties."

*　　*　　*　　*　　*　　*
45

This went on for many months as Julie abandoned men for women. Through Suzie, she met a number of bi and lesbian women, and became both active and passive.

I lost count of the number of cunts she tasted. I got tribbed, fingered, dildoed and done with a strapon so many times. I began to think this was to be the way it was for the rest of my life. I missed the hot, throbbing, insistent, rawness of the male.

Chapter 10

The return of the rod

Julie had lost touch a bit with her old friends. One night her school friend Pam, the one who had introduced her to sex, phoned to announce that she was getting married and wanted Julie to come to the reception.

"Of course, I'd love to come," Julie replied. "It's been so long since I saw you. So much must have happened to both of us."

"I heard about your break up," Pam said in a concerned tone.

"I'm glad to be away from him," Julie responded. "Life is so much better now. So why has it taken so long for you to find a husband?"

"Long story. We'll catch up later."

*　*　*　*　*　*

For the party, Julie thought she should dress classic, so she put on a tight-fitting tube dress, wore sheer stockings and her gold heels. Tasteful. The reception was in a large hotel on the outskirts of the city.

She arrived about half an hour late. She knew it was always better not to get to these events too early as the crowd would not have then built up, and she might end up having to talk with some boring relative.

After having to talk to a number of Pam's tedious relatives, eventually, Julie found a seat at the bar. A rather tasty young man introduced himself as Pam's cousin. I could feel Julie responding to him.

'What is going on?' I wondered, as a rush of hormones sends a signal for me to get prepared.

I am slowly becoming lubricated.

Things appear to be going well at the top level as they openly flirt. Only a few minutes later, he leads Julie to the door. They are going to 'get a breath of air'. I am anticipating some heavy breathing. The young man leads Julie behind a storage unit where they cannot be seen.

He pushes her against the wall, and some intense kissing begins. I become totally lubricated, which is very timely as I feel his fingers trying to navigate their way around Julie's panties. The fingertips quickly slip into my slit, the gully that leads to my opening.

"You're nice and juicy," he announces.

Julie reaches down, rolls her tube skirt almost up to her waist and starts pulling her panties away from me. They get to her knees before he bends and takes over the task. So now, I am readied as a target.

She opens her legs as far as she can in this standing position. Six months with only fingers and dildoes is about to end. I feel the head sliding in my slit seeking for my opening. I wasn't expecting this at all when we left for the reception. I just thought Julie would get drunk, then return home for some vigorous masturbation with Miss Clitty.

It's in. He gives a huge thrust, and I feel his cock slide as far inside me as it can get in this position.

"Lovely and tight," he says.

Well, I should be after six months of being left on the shelf. I can assure him, that if he does this every night for a month or so, I will be as easy to slide in as cunts can get.

The thrusting starts. His cockhead slips up and down in my first three inches. Getting used like this is the best thing ever. I tense and relax in unison with the thrusts. This cock is clearly very experienced and knows how to make the best of any position, even a difficult one like this.

"Trust me, Julie," I hear the man say. "I can hold you."

His hands go under her buttocks and start to support her weight. She lifts her legs up and opens them wide.

The cockhead now tastes the innermost parts of my chamber. It's so good feeling it going that far in. His rod now uses my full length, sliding in and out at a good speed. I must say I would like it a bit faster, but this will do. I've been cock-starved for half-a-year, so I won't be making any demands.

Julie is whimpering and groaning. She's enjoying this as much as I am.

"Yer a fucking good cunt, Julie," her paramour announces, as he rams in and out of me.

'I'm one of the best cunt's going,' I tell his cockhead.

'You sure are. Almost as good as the redhead last week,' he teases.

I'll show him. I start to tense my muscles, gripping around his shaft lower down. If I could just contract my muscles deep inside, that would probably be a winner, but I have not yet learned how to do this, or if it was even possible.

'My balls are sending me the tingles. They want to cum,' his cockhead confides.

'So soon,' I say disappointed.

'I'll try and hold back, but balls will be balls. When they are ready, it's all over. Nothing I can do about it.'

There's a series of quick movements, followed by a large gasp, and a powerful thrust which pushes him as far into me as he can go. His shaft twitches and I feel his cockhead spurting out its juice about ten times in succession. There's a lot of it too. Warm and clingy. Mrs womb will be happy. We haven't been bathed in spunk for ages.

His cockhead says goodbye abruptly as his master pull's out. He's finished having fun, and no doubt wants to get back to the party.

Julie's feet are back on the ground. She's gasping with the effort of taking a banging. Unfortunately, it didn't last long enough for me to even think of being able to give her an orgasm. She fusses about in her bag, finding tissues to wipe off the sticky stuff that's leaking out. There was a lot of it, so I hope she doesn't run out of tissues. She puts her panties on again and stuffs them with some tissues in the hope of capturing the rest of his mess which is still high up inside me.

She can't face going back to the party, so goes to the hotel reception and gets them to call her a taxi.

*   *   *   *   *   *

When we get home, Julie gets into a warm bath, and Miss Clitty gets vigorously used, till she gives Julie an orgasm.

The next day Julie, gets up early and visits the chemist for a pill to ensure she is not going to become a mum. She decides to make an appointment with her doctor to resume her regular contraceptive pill, which she had given up during her adventures with the girls.

I now know I am to be a core part of her sexual activity again. I make a promise to always try very hard to give her an orgasm, even if the guy is inept, selfish or comes too soon.

Chapter 11

Doubling up

Julie is wondering how she can meet more men. She remembers that one of her friends, Cathy, often went clubbing to pick up guys. Her number is in her phone, so later in the evening, she calls her up.

"Hi, Cath. You still doing the clubs?"

"Yeah. Most Friday and Saturday nights."

"You get to meet some neat guys?"

"Sure. There's plenty of beef for the taking."

Julie laughs.

"Can I tag along sometime?"

"You missing it after you split up? How long's it been?"

"Eight months, till last night."

"What were you up to last night?"

"Was at Pam's wedding. Got familiar with her cousin."

"Got familiar!" Cathy laughed. "Legs apart at midnight was it?"

"You got it, exactly."

"I know some guys that we might be able to pick up. I expect they will be in the Blue Cavern night club on Friday."

"What are they like?"

"Cocks on legs. They're no great lookers, but they

have what it takes for a good night."

"Cocks?"

"Stamina."

"They last a while?"

"Ad infinitum," Cathy giggles.

"Count me in for half an hour of that."

"I'll give them a call to let them know we'll be there."

*　*　*　*　*　*

Julie and Cathy meet up in a pub close to the club.

"Let's have a few drinks first before diving into the Blue Cavern," Cathy suggests.

"Night out, is it girls?" an older guy says, as they make their way, bearing drinks, through the crowded bar to find an empty space in which to stand.

"Yeah," Cathy replies in a curt tone.

He doesn't get the implied message, but tags along with them.

"You married and looking for a bit of fun?" he asks.

"No."

"So, you're not married, but still looking for a bit of fun?"

He is trying hard.

"Let me buy you nice girls some drinks, and we will see where it goes."

"Yeah, we'd love that."

He goes off to the bar.

"Right, now's our chance for a sharp exit."

Julie and Cathy sneak to the door and slip out into the night.

They make their way to the Blue Cavern club, which is in the next street. Julie checks over her shoulder to make sure that guy is not following them.

51

The club is a large space painted light blue at the top and dark blue lower down. It's already quite busy. It takes Julie a few minutes to get used to the loud disco music and the ever-moving lights.

"Let's find a seat so we can scope out the talent," Cathy suggests.

There are lots of younger guys prancing about. Julie looks at their tight trousers, and wonders if she might be able to get off with any of them.

Cathy points out a guy who is showing off his dancing skills.

"Look at the bum on that," she giggles. "He can wiggle that between my thighs any time."

I sense an excitement developing in Julie, not quite a flood of hormones, but definitely a growing tension. I begin to slowly lubricate.

The two of them sit for a while, sharing comments about the guys that pass by.

Cathy is suddenly animated.

"I see them. Over at the bar."

She points them out to Julie, then gets out her phone.

"We're round the back at a table," she tells him. "Bring us some double voddies."

Once they get to the table, they focus their attention on Julie.

"Nice eyes and even nicer thighs," the taller one, Jason, giggles.

"You as easy, as your mate?" the other, who's called Billy, asks, but does not expect an answer, immediately turning to Cathy. "How many times is it now, Cathy? You still not tired of us?"

"She likes it too much," Jason suggests. "What's it to be, then? Back to your place, Cath, or do we split up?"

"We'll have to toss to see who gets Julie then," his

mate laughs.

"Let's stick together. You like swapping over, Julie?"

Poor Julie is embarrassed and mumbles incoherently.

"I'll take that for a yes, then."

I'm now dribbling enough juice out to wet my lips. I realise I'm soon going to service two cocks. What a delicious thought.

They leave the club. Cathy and Julie walk arm in arm down the pavement, flanked by Jason and Billy.

Billy pulls Julie into a shop doorway and pins her against the wall. I feel him grind his crotch against me. His hand is up Julie's skirt, and he pushes her panties into her slit. I get a little thrill from the pressure.

"Cathy's got some great looking friends. You're effing gorgeous. I could take you up a back lane and give you a right good time."

"Come on, you two. Stop messing about." His taller friend says. "Let's push on to Cathy's place."

"I just fancied a quick sample."

"Let's just pass on the starters and move on to the main course. I'm sure that's okay with Cath and Julie."

As soon as we get into Cathy's flat, she starts stripping off, throwing her clothes onto the sofa.

"Cath's keen tonight," Jason says.

"So am I," Billy laughs, unzipping and letting his cock hang out his jeans.

I am now disgracefully liquid.

Julie joins in the stripping party.

When she starts to roll her stockings down her thighs, Billy requests, "No keep them on. Stockings are a right turn-on."

Julie is eying up the two, now fully erect, penises. My entrance is completely soaked. There will be no resistance when they slide in.

Cath leads us to her bedroom, and she and Julie lie side by side on the bed. Her legs are open, so I am visible to the two guys.

There's to be no foreplay, not even a fingering.

A cockhead is immediately pressing against me. Julie's thighs widen to give it full access. He gives a big thrust, and I feel it slide in a few inches.

"Tight, fucking pussy," the cock's owner, Billy, tells everyone.

I try to let myself go as loose as possible as Billy gives me a series of short stabbing strokes.

"Let me have a go. See what it's like," Jason asks.

Suddenly, the cock pulls out and leaves me. Julie lets out a groan.

The two guys swap places on the bed, and I sense the imminent arrival of the second cock.

It's rubbing against my opening, spreading my juices over its head.

Julie gasps as it pushes inside me.

It's a big one. I feel it forcing its way inside me. It's stretching me. It's very thick. Jason holds his rod still inside me for almost a minute, marking time. I feel the blood pulsing in his cock.

The bed begins to bounce. Cathy's cunt is now getting vigorously pounded. I need some of that soon, myself. Jason's cock, responding to his mate's shagging, now starts to move.

I love it when they slide in the full length, and not just poke in my entrance. He is thick, but I can easily take his full length. I can tell he's a very experienced cock. Lots of legs must have opened for him, as he knows what we cunts like.

Julie is getting the full pleasure. She likes it so much better lying down on a bed, to standing up leaning against a wall.

The bouncing on the bed slows down as Billy now changes to slowly stirring Cathy's cunt. Cathy clearly approves of the different rhythm, as she mumbles encouragement to Billy.

Jason decides to take the lead now. He suddenly starts thrusting fast and furious. I am taken aback at the speed of it. His cockhead slides the full six inches up and down inside me. Julie cries out. The wee darling is having so much fun. I must try and give her an orgasm. This guy will probably last long enough for me to get fully excited.

"Swap now, Jason," Billy shouts.

The lovely thick rod, which I am just getting used to, pulls out of me, and I feel Julie's sexual tension crash down. But within a few seconds, the two guys have changed over, and I am getting re-acquainted with Billy's cock.

Julie is determined to get an orgasm. She slips her hand down her belly and locates her fingertips on Miss Clitty.

Billy's cock is clearly taken with me. It slides my full length. It's experienced enough not to slip out on the out-stroke. That would mess Julie up, as I know she needs continual stimulation on her path to the climax.

I'm uncertain if the swapping is over, but it seems likely, judging by the way the bed is being bounced by Jason and Cathy, whose cunt is certainly getting the full works. Intense and fast. Billy's cock seems to throb and even lengthen a bit, as he hears his mate getting close to the magic moment.

"Fuck," Jason calls out, and the bed suddenly stops moving. He groans a few times, and I know Cathy's cunt is getting filled with the white juice. Billy slows down as he listens to the climax. I'll be getting the same soon.

"I bet that was effing good, man," Billy says.

"Yeah, I really needed a hard shag. Well, you know what Cathy is like," Jason confides. "Well, Cathy, was that a bit of alright or not?"

"Seven out of ten," she teases. "You lost points for cuming too quick."

"We'll make up for that later, won't we Billy? The first one takes the edge off of it, and then we can go on for hours. I've got at least three stiffies in me tonight, maybe more. What about you Billy?"

"I'm still just getting warmed up."

"Let's get off the bed and let these two use the full space. Julie needs room to spread her great thighs wide. Isn't that so, Julie? Anyway, I want to get a good view of things," Jason smirks.

I'll have to be on my best behaviour if I am going to be closely watched. Billy and Julie adjust their position on the bed. His cock manages, despite their changing position, to remain rooted inside me. It's clearly determined not to leave me until the inevitable finish.

Billy starts to stir his cock inside me. Long slow strokes. Julie's fingers work themselves on Miss Clitty. I feel the tension begin to build. Julie's thighs lift up from the bed, and I feel the change of angle. Billy's cock is now moving almost vertically. This is a good way. Cocks call it 'piledriving', and it sure feels nice. Julie is now gasping uncontrollably. Her fingertips have taken her close to the edge.

Billy senses what's happening inside Julie. "That's it girl, have a cum. Let me finish you off."

His cock now wildly thrusts in and out of me.

Miss Clitty has taken Julie as far as she can, so she bows out and leaves the finish to me. I'm so excited now that I twitch my muscles on each inward stroke of the cock. She lets out a long groan, her hips thrust upwards three times, then I feel her thighs begin to quiver. I release all the tension that's been thrust into me, and Julie cries out, as her orgasm takes over and her arms and legs thrash about.

'God, she can cum. Bet you wish you could have one of those, Cathy,' I hear Jason whisper.

Billy's cock clearly needs his fun too. Julie lowers her legs and lets them fall wide open. Unlike Miss Clitty, who wants one to stop once she's unloaded her sexual energy, I can go on and on. Cunts can take it.

Billy bounces his bum up and down, driving his cock hard into me.

"Come on, give her it fast. The girlies like that," Jason suggests.

Billy's cock, who I have got to know quite well, wants to bury his head as deep inside me as he can get. I know just how to give a cock a good time, as I open and then tense, in lockstep with Billy's thrusting. I am so saturated with my juices now that I make those lovely sloppy sounds as he moves in me.

Julie groans, clearly loving the post-orgasmic sex. I'm so relaxed now, letting Billy use me as he will. His cockhead seems to enlarge, and the shaft becomes even harder and more insistent in its movements.

I've lost count of how long this has been going on. It's probably at least two or three times what Jason gave Cathy.

The shaft stops pounding, pushes as far into me as it will go, then Billy shouts and grunts with the exertion. I feel a small pulse of spunk, then the shaft pulls the head down towards my opening, reverses and quickly pushes in again. This time I feel a powerful spray into me, then the cock moves up and down me, pumping out spunk on each in-stroke. I am sexually baptised.

Billy collapses on top of Julie. Happily, he does not immediately pull out of me as Jason had done with Cathy, but lets his cock gradually lose its stiffness and slip out naturally.

Jason breaks the gentle coming-down mood "Great pair of fannies. I bet you had a wank earlier, Billy. You lasted ages. No need for a wank now with these two spreading their legs for us."

He comes over and lies beside Julie on the bed. He takes her hand and moves it to his crotch.

"Watching you has got my pecker up. Bet you could take it again, right now."

I feel his fingertips at my opening, playing with the juice and the spunk which is now seeping out. I let Julie know I want more prick. She responds by widening her legs, and a few seconds later, I am giving a big warm, slippery, sloppy welcome to Jason's totally hard rod.

Julie is greedy for orgasms, and gets her fingertips again onto Miss Clitty. The big thick cock fills me nicely, and I let Julie know I want much more of this.

Over about two hours Julie excels herself with three loud orgasms, which totally endears her to the guys.

Chapter 12

Epilogue

The night was a turning point. Julie realised that she could take control of her orgasms. When she was with her lesbian friends, they always made sure she had a good orgasm, usually a series of them.

Men were very different. It was more hit and miss. Even the more sensitive men, once they got close to their own cum, became so taken up with it that they just selfishly used me. That I did not mind one bit, as I just loved the feeling of them sliding inside me, but for Julie, she often felt she was being used.

She had found the answer. She would bring on her cum by using her fingertips, while the man was shagging away, oblivious, on top of her.

This meant I had to work together with Miss Clitty. We were to be a team - the cum team. For years we had resented each other. I always felt Julie preferred her to me, while Miss Clitty was jealous of the way Julie enjoyed my being fingered or given the cock.

Now we were to act as one, to make sure Julie got her fair share of the thrills. Luckily, Jason had become attached to Julie and visited her two or three nights a week. This gave Clitty and me the chance to hone our act, so after a few weeks, Julie was getting some astoundingly good orgasms.

Not that she abandoned her women friends. She loved the different tone of the orgasms with them. Soft and subtle, as opposed to riding a bucking bronco. She needed both, and there were enough days in the week to fill.

I became quite attached to Miss Clitty. She can be quite stuck-up, superior and precious, but when we worked together, we made great sex music. She always saw me as 'her downstairs', the working-class skivvy, polishing cockheads. I was so messy compared with her gentility, even though she did like a taste of spunk occasionally. Some men liked to rub their cockhead against her, which she took a particular delight in.

Clitty and I became great friends, the two sides of Julie's sexual nature. From then on, we were the orgasm team, and Julie loved us both equally.